To Mary, who listened all the way through
A.F. & P.P.

For Jane
K.L.

Library of Congress Cataloging-in-Publication
data is on file with the publisher.

Text copyright © 2014 Andrew Fusek Peters and Polly Peters
Pictures copyright © 2014 Karin Littlewood
First published in Great Britain in 2014 by Wayland,
a division of Hachette Children's Group, UK
Published in 2015 by Albert Whitman & Company
ISBN 978-0-8075-1273-9

Printed in China
10 9 8 7 6 5 4 3 2 1 WKT 20 19 18 17 16 15

For more information about Albert Whitman & Company,
visit our web site at www.albertwhitman.com.

The COLOR THIEF

A family's story of depression

written by
Andrew Fusek Peters
& Polly Peters

illustrated by
Karin Littlewood

Albert Whitman & Company
Chicago, Illinois

My dad's life was full of color.
Every day, clouds smiled at him and trees waved hello.
We went walking together. We saw green hills
snoozing in the afternoon light and
bright flowers singing to the sun.

But one day, Dad was full of sadness,
all the way to the top.
He said his sky had turned gray.

I thought I had done something wrong,
but he told me I hadn't.

Soon every day became a sad day for Dad.
He only saw the sun sulking, clouds
frowning, rain crying. We didn't go walking.
We didn't do anything together anymore.

Outside, the trees stood silently, shaking their heads.
Dad stayed inside and looked out the window.

He said that if he went out, the lampposts
would laugh at him or the streets would call him names.

I thought I had done something wrong, but he told me I hadn't.

He said that all the colors were gone.
Someone had stolen them away; just taken them
one by one. He said he felt sad and stuck,
like a marble in a bottle.

When the phone rang,
he told it to go away.

When the doorbell buzzed,
he pretended not to hear it.

I gave him hugs.
We all gave him hugs.
But he put those hugs
away in a box.

Then he closed the curtains
and stayed in bed all day.

I thought I had done something wrong, but he told me I hadn't.

I felt lonely. There was a heavy
feeling inside me and I missed my dad.
I missed the sound of his laugh and his smiling eyes.

I drew a picture of him inside a big ice cube.

Dad went to see important people at a hospital.
They told him he was very ill and gave him medicine for his mind.
And they found him someone to talk to,
someone who listened.

Days turned over slowly,
one page at a time.
Weeks rumbled past our front door.
Months were stretchy,
like chewing gum.

And then one day, Dad opened the
window and the sun crept into our house.
I made a cup of tea for him,
and he said it tasted good.

The gray shadows in the corners of
the room grew smaller…and smaller.

I asked Dad if he
wanted to go for a little walk.
He said yes and I held his hand.

The sky winked a blue eye.
Clouds smiled and every
tree waved hello.

Dad looked around. Then he looked down at me
and picked me up in a great, big, squeezy hug.

My dad was back.

He smiled and the colors were bright all around us.